PENGUIN PROBLEMS

BY JORY JOHN ILLUSTRATED BY LANE SMITH

WALKER BOOKS
AND SUBSIDIARIES
LONDON · BOSTON · SYDNEY · AUCKLAND

To Alyssa and my mom, Deborah
~ J.J.

To Sylvie
~ L.S.

First published in Great Britain 2016 by Walker Books Ltd
87 Vauxhall Walk, London SE11 5HJ

10 9 8 7 6 5 4 3 2 1

Text © 2016 Jory John   Illustrations © 2016 Lane Smith

Published by arrangement with Random House Children's Books,
a division of Penguin Random House LLC, New York, U.S.A.

This book has been typeset in Gill Sans

Printed in China

British Library Cataloguing in Publication Data:
a catalogue record for this book is available from the British Library

ISBN 978-1-4063-7599-2

www.walker.co.uk

It's way too early.

My beak is cold.

What's with all the squawking, you guys?

It snowed some more last night,
and I don't even like the snow.

It's too bright out here.

I'm hungry.

I'd like a fish.

Where are all the fish?!

HEY!

FISH!

GET OUT HERE!

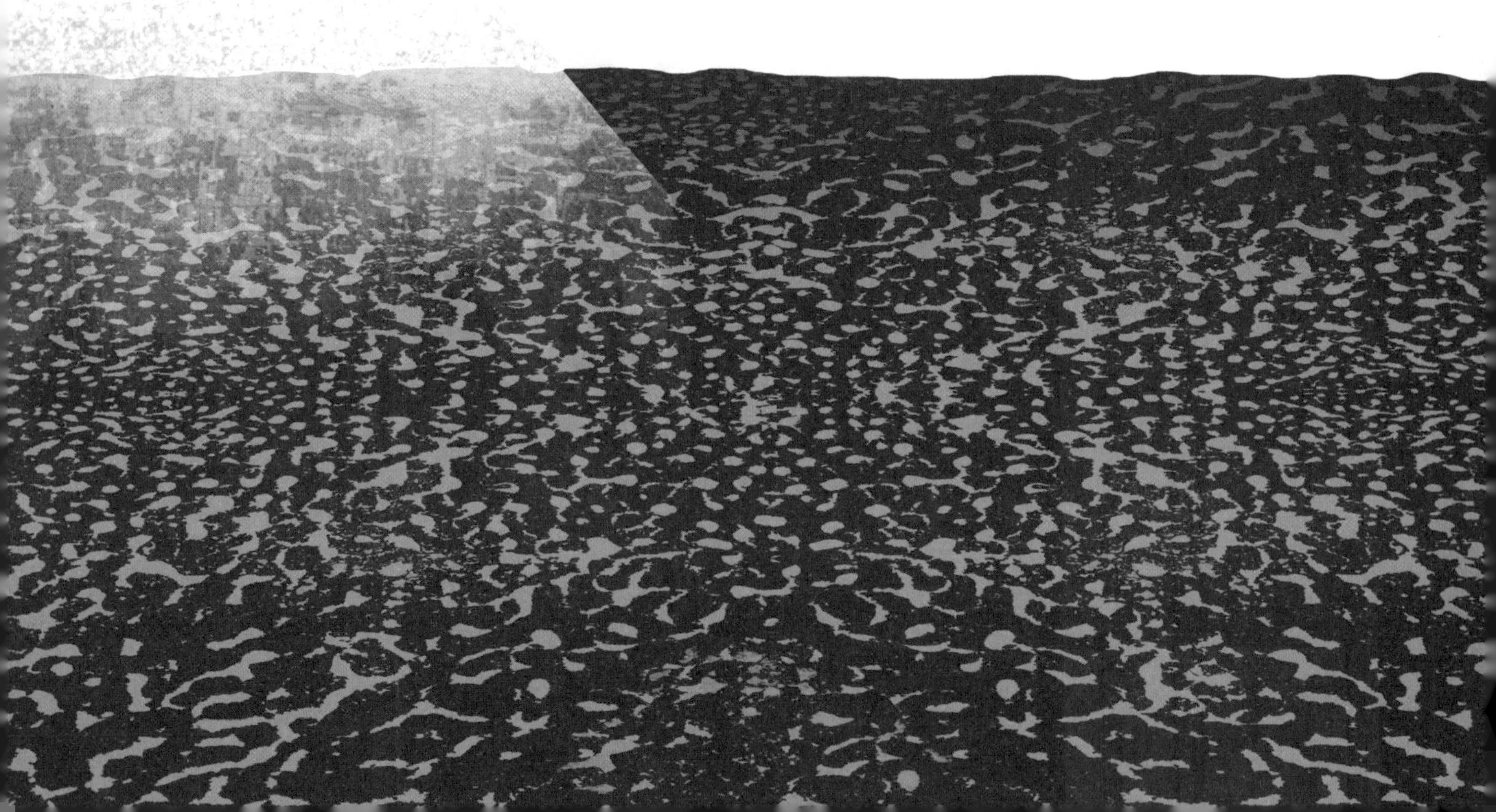

The ocean smells too salty today.

I'm not buoyant enough.
I sink like a stupid rock.

It's way too dark down here.

Brrrr!

I said, brrrrrrrrrrrrrrrrr!

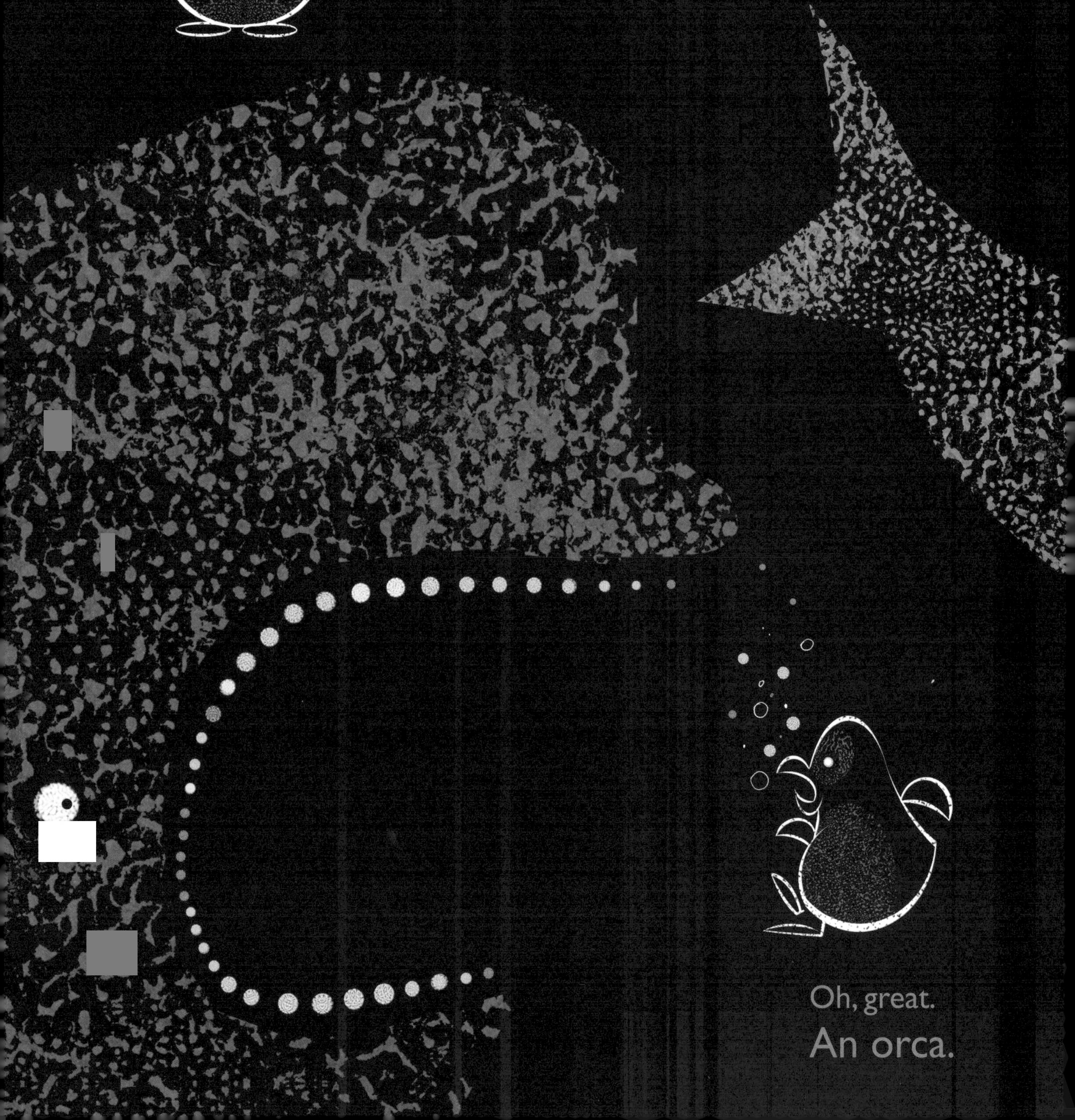

Oh, great.
An orca.

Oh, great.
A leopard seal.

Oh, great.
A shark.

What *is* it with this place?

I don't like being hunted.

I'm still hungry, but my flippers ache.

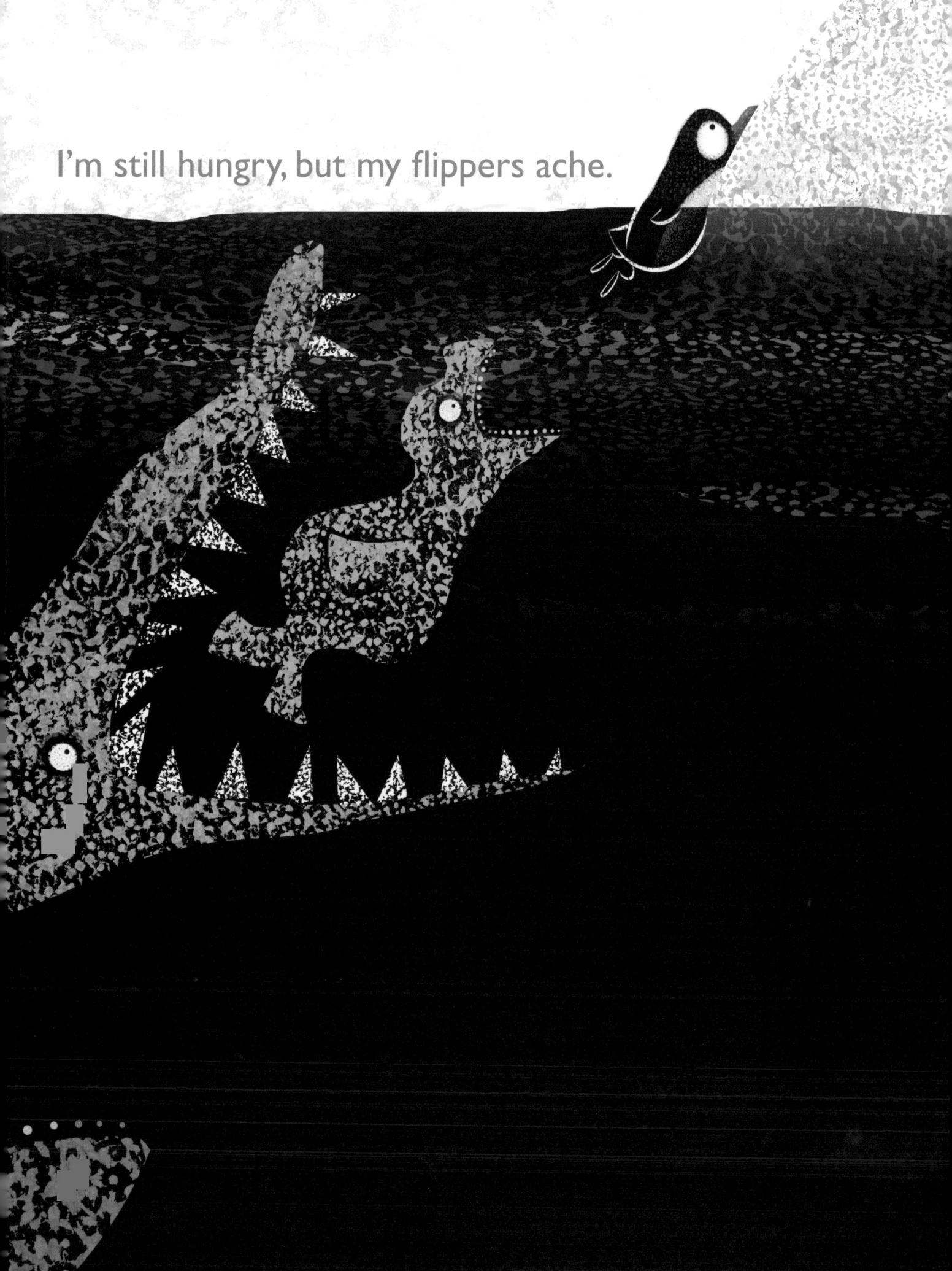

I waddle too much. I look silly when I waddle.

See?

I wish I could fly, but I can't.

See?

Everybody looks the same as me.

I look the same as everybody else.

I have so many problems!

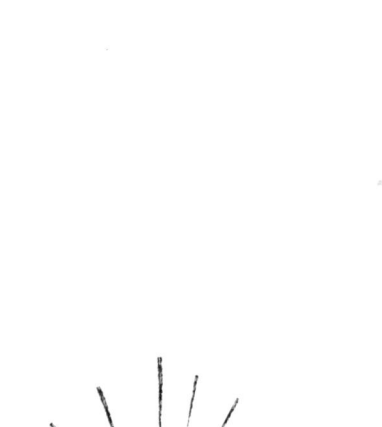

And nobody even cares!

Excuse me, sir?

What?!

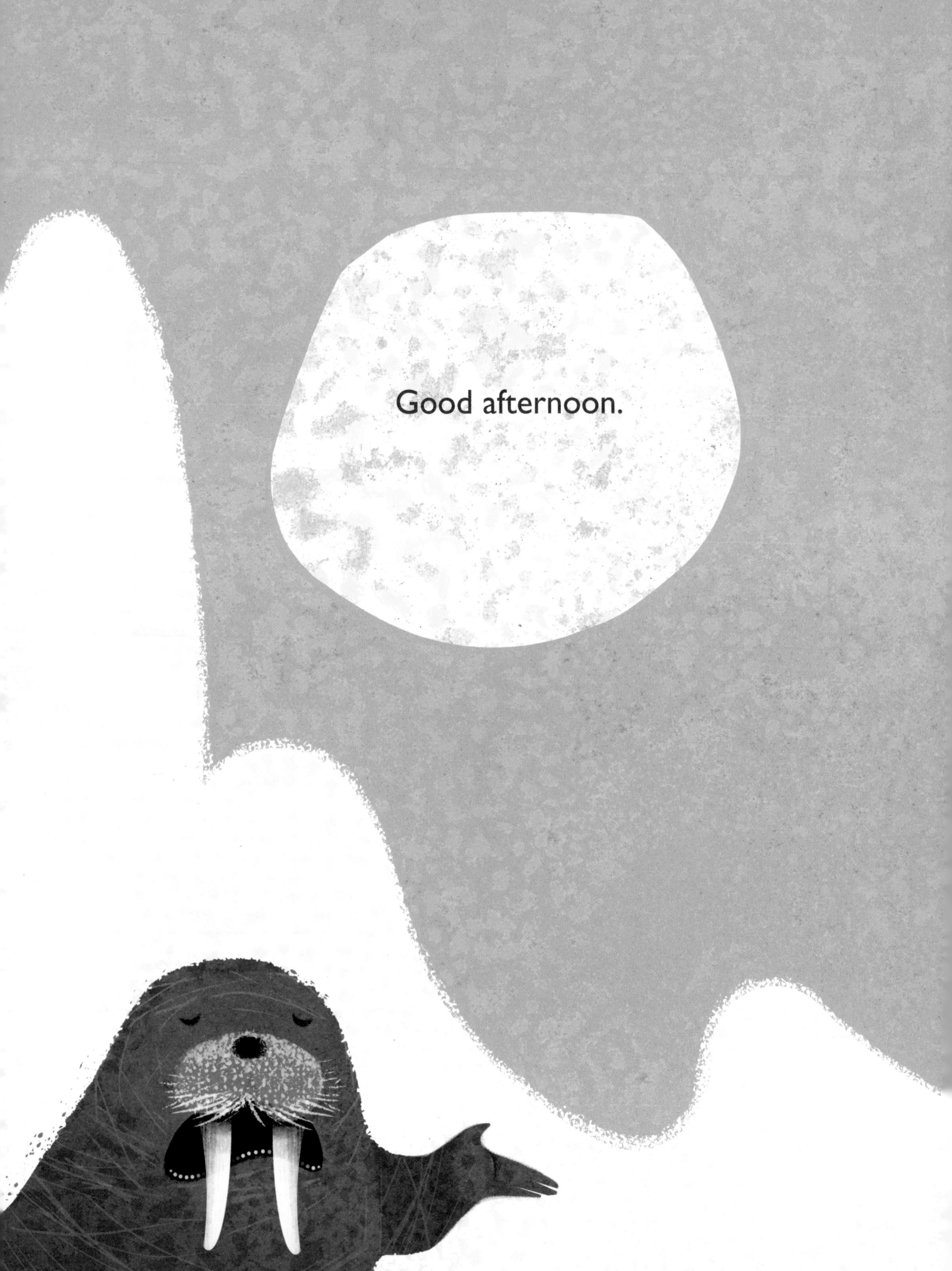

I sense that today has been difficult, but lo! Look around you, Penguin. Have you noticed the way the mountains are reflected in the ocean like a painting? Have you gazed upon the blue of that cloudless, winter sky, my friend? Have you felt the sun as it gently warms your back? Have you simply stood with your penguin brothers and sisters and elders, who adore you?

Yes, some things are challenging out here. Yes, we all have difficult moments, from the walruses to the polar bears, from the whales to the penguins. But hear me now, my new friend: I wouldn't trade my life for any other, and I am quite sure you wouldn't, either. I am certain that when you think about it, you'll realize that you are exactly where you need to be.

Please think about what I've said, Penguin.

Goodbye for now.

Who on earth *was* that guy?!
Why do strangers always talk to me?
Walruses don't understand *penguin problems*!

Sigh.
OK, OK.

Maybe that walrus has a point.
After all, I *do* love the mountains.

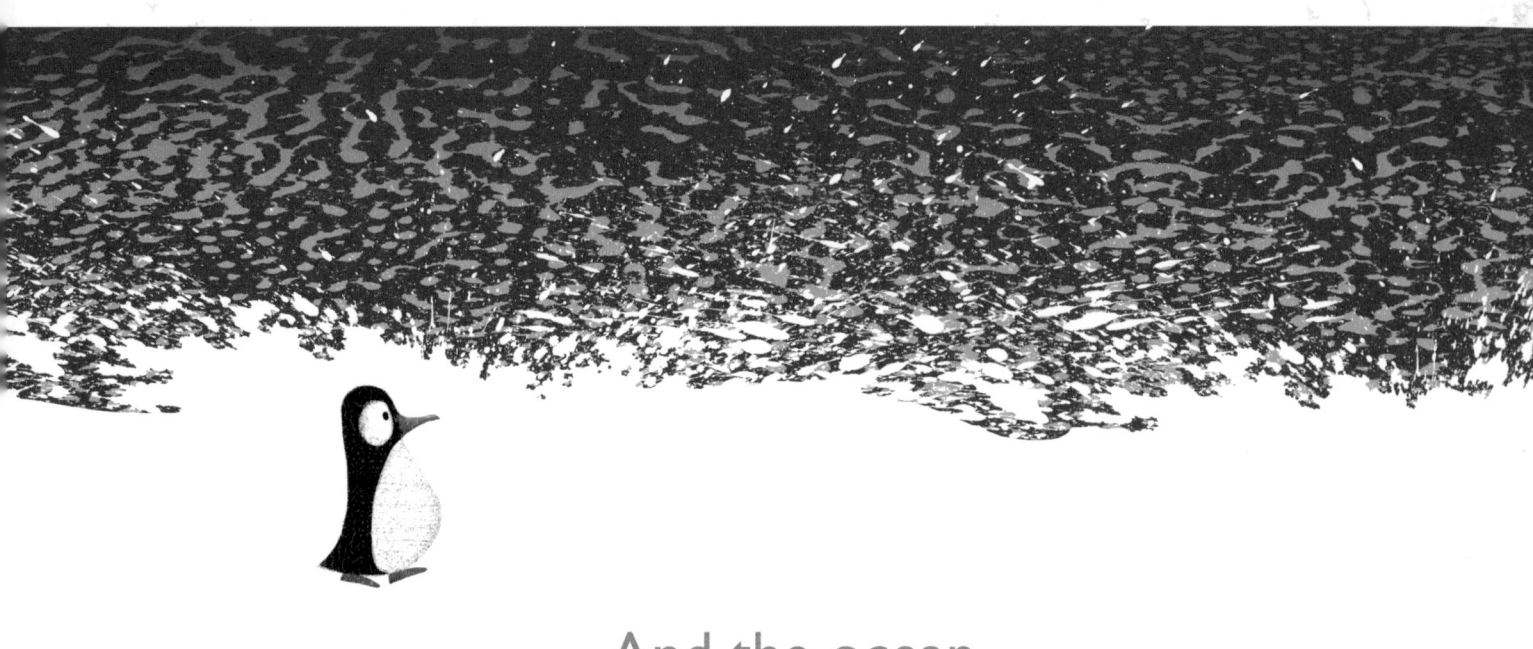

And the ocean.

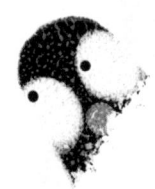

And the sky.
And I have friends and family.
This is my only home, and this is my only life.
Maybe things will work out, after all.

My beak is cold.

It gets dark way too early.